CAN YOU NET
THE LOCH NESS MONSTER?

AN INTERACTIVE MONSTER HUNT

BY BRANDON TERRELL AND MATT DOEDEN

CAPSTONE PRESS
a capstone imprint

Published by Capstone Press, an imprint of Capstone.
1710 Roe Crest Drive
North Mankato, Minnesota 56003
capstonepub.com

Library of Congress Cataloging-in-Publication Data
Names: Terrell, Brandon, 1978- author. | Doeden, Matt, author.
Title: Can you net the Loch Ness Monster? : an interactive monster hunt /
  by Brandon Terrell and Matt Doeden.
Description: North Mankato, MN : Capstone Press, 2021. | Series: You choose:
  monster hunter | Includes bibliographical references. | Audience: Ages 8–11. |
  Audience: Grades 4–6.
Identifiers: LCCN 2021012695 (print) | LCCN 2021012696 (ebook) |
  ISBN 9781663907677 (hardcover) | ISBN 9781663920317 (paperback) |
  ISBN 9781663907646 (ebook PDF)
Subjects: LCSH: Loch Ness monster—Juvenile fiction. | Monsters—Juvenile
  fiction. | Plot-your-own stories. | CYAC: Loch Ness monster—Fiction. |
  Monsters—Fiction. | Plot-your-own stories. | LCGFT: Choose-your-own stories.
Classification: LCC PZ7.T273 Cal 2021 (print) | LCC PZ7.T273 (ebook) |
  DDC 813.6 [Fic]—dc23
LC record available at https://lccn.loc.gov/2021012695
LC ebook record available at https://lccn.loc.gov/2021012696

Summary: New evidence keeps coming in. A grainy photo appears to show Scotland's famous Loch Ness Monster. A blurry video seems to show a similar beast in New York State. A report from Africa mentions yet another lake monster. Does this evidence prove that stories about legendary lake monsters around the world are real? It's up to YOU to find out! With dozens of choices, you can follow the clues to the end. Which path will YOU CHOOSE to discover the truth?

Editorial Credits
Editor: Aaron Sautter; Designer: Bobbie Nuytten; Media Researcher: Kelly Garvin;
Production Specialist: Laura Manthe

Image Credits
Getty Images: gremlin, 69, Keystone, 104, Ludovic Debono, 6, Print Collector, 102, Vaara, 32; Newscom: Steve Challice/Cover Images, 35; Shutterstock: Alberto Loyo, 90, Alexander Armitage, 10, Alizada Studios, 20, Almazoff, 93, anastas_styles, 24, BHamms, 48, Bob Pool, 63, buchandbee, 106, Elegant Solution, 107, Ercan Uc, 83, Fabian Salamanca, 44, Fabio Gomes Freitas, 41, Grobler du Preez, 85, Guy Banville, 55, Jan Miko, 52, Kariakin Aleksandr, 107, Kyle Towns, 57, Laci Gibbs, 19, Magicleaf, 106, Mark Pitt Images, 79, Milton Louiz, 86, Mysikrysa, 26, Ondrej Prosicky, 98, scubadesign, 28, Sergey Uryadnikov, 74, Sleepy Joe, 72, SofART, 106, 107, Stubblefield Photography, 38, Sunshine Seeds, 96, Victor Habbick, Cover, Zastolskiy Victor, 59, 66, Zdenka Mlynarikova, 13, Zhenyakot, 107

All internet sites appearing in back matter were available and accurate when this book was sent to press.

TABLE OF CONTENTS

ABOUT YOUR ADVENTURE

YOU are a museum worker who has an interest in cryptozoology. You enjoy studying evidence of strange, legendary creatures from old tales around the world. When you see reports pop up about sightings of the famous Loch Ness Monster and similar creatures, you can't wait to go on an adventure and see them for yourself. Will you be able to find proof that the legendary beasts are real?

Chapter One sets the scene. Then you choose which path to read. Follow the directions at the bottom of the page as you read the stories. The decisions you make will change your outcome. After you finish one path, go back and read the others for new perspectives and more adventures.

Turn the page to begin your adventure.

Shadowy shapes seen through the fog on Loch Ness may often be mistaken for the Loch Ness Monster.

CHAPTER 1

SOMETHING IS STIRRING

"Whoa, check this out!" shouts Aliah. You look up from your laptop, where you're writing a paper about the mysterious Bigfoot.

Aliah, your roommate and best friend, sits on the couch staring at her phone. She holds it up for you to see. It's a blurry picture of some sort. You can see water and a dark shape. But it's hard to tell just what you're looking at.

"Someone snapped this photo of something huge just below the water's surface," Aliah explains. "Do you think it might be real?"

Aliah knows about your passion for cryptozoology—the study of creatures whose existence has not been proven.

Turn the page.

You volunteer at a cryptid museum, teaching the public about how such creatures might live, eat, and stay out of sight. Aliah usually just rolls her eyes when you bring up your favorite subject. She's not a believer. But this has caught her eye.

"Hold on, let me check something," you answer. You open your web browser on your laptop and go to your favorite cryptozoology message board. Sure enough, the photo is the talk of the board.

"This is it! Real proof of the Loch Ness Monster!" announces one message.

"Let them prove us wrong now!" reads another.

More messages talk about recent sightings of other lake monsters. One message includes a grainy video clip of Champ in New York State. Another talks about reports from Africa of some villagers who saw a beast called Mokele-mbembe (muh-KAY-lay em-BEM-bay).

"Okay, I'm officially interested," you say, leaning in to read more. Ancient, dinosaur-like creatures living in deep freshwater lakes are the holy grail of cryptid hunters. You've researched Bigfoot for years. But the reports of mysterious lake monsters have really grabbed your attention.

You can feel the excitement building inside you. It's not a decision of *if* you'll go on an expedition to find Nessie or another lake monster. It's just a matter of how soon you can leave.

You close the page for the message board and open a new one to shop for a plane ticket. Which creature are you going to look for?

To travel to Scotland to search for the Loch Ness Monster, turn to page 11.

To fly to New York to look for Champ, turn to page 45.

To book a trip to Africa to seek out Mokele-mbembe, turn to page 75.

On a dark, cloudy day, it's easy to imagine a large, mysterious creature that lurks in the depths of Loch Ness in Scotland.

CHAPTER 2
SEARCHING FOR NESSIE

Nessie may be the most famous cryptid in the world. For more than 100 years, people have reported seeing—something—in the deep waters of Loch Ness in Scotland. You can't resist the chance to find one of the world's most famous cryptid creatures. You book your flight and pack your bags for the adventure of a lifetime.

During your long flight to Inverness, Scotland, you research as much as you can about the recent Nessie sighting. The man who snapped the photo is named Donal McFadden. McFadden isn't hard to find. He lives just a few miles from the lake. He runs a small shop that sells Nessie souvenirs to tourists. You need to talk to him.

Turn the page.

You rent a car and make your way toward the famous lake. The countryside is beautiful. Rolling green hills, open fields, and mist-covered forests dot the landscape. By the time you reach McFadden's shop, it's late afternoon.

You park the car and walk inside. A little bell jingles as you enter. At first, the shop appears empty. There aren't any customers. The shelves are filled with Nessie toys, books, and postcards. A big inflatable Nessie hangs over the counter.

"Hello?" you call out. You hear a rustling in the back.

A tall man with a mop of wild red hair steps through a door. "Hello, lad," he says. "Welcome to my shop. Can I interest you in some fine books on our famous monster?"

"McFadden?" you ask.

"Aye," he answers, nodding.

Turn to page 14.

Loch Ness is a popular destination for tourists. Each year, many people travel there to either search for Nessie or to enjoy the lake's scenic views.

You introduce yourself, explaining that you're a cryptid hunter who saw his photograph online. "I'd really like to see where you took the photo," you explain.

McFadden is friendly at first. But as you talk, he grows nervous. He keeps looking over his shoulder. It seems like he just wants you gone.

"Please," you say. "I just need a little help. If you won't show me, would you at least point me in the right direction?"

McFadden's shoulders slump. "Then I'm afraid I have to point you back home, lad." he says. "I never meant for my photo to get so much attention. I wish I'd never done it."

"Done what?" you ask.

McFadden sighs. "The photo is fake. I made it on my computer. Business has been slow. I just thought . . . maybe a photo would get people interested in finding Nessie again. It was a bad idea. I'm sorry."

To head back to the airport to go home, turn to page 16.

To stay in Scotland and continue your search alone, turn to page 23.

Your heart sinks. You kick yourself for getting your hopes up. You're supposed to be an expert on cryptids, but you just got fooled by a hoax. The bell above the door jingles loudly as you storm out.

Before heading back to the airport, you give Aliah a call. "I'm heading home," you tell her. "It was a dead end. I was a fool to even come."

"Keep your head up," she tells you. "At least you followed your dreams. Maybe next time."

With that, you're back on the road. You blast some music to drown out your sorrow. You're so mad that you can't even enjoy the beautiful scenery around you.

Suddenly, a pickup truck speeds up behind you. The driver honks the horn and flashes the lights. You stick your hand out the window to wave him by. But he keeps honking. You peer into your mirror. Is that McFadden?

You pull over. The pickup pulls up behind you. McFadden hops out and steps to your window.

"I'm so sorry," he says. "I didn't want to say it at first, but . . . I owe you this. I faked the photo, but what I saw was real. Nessie is real, and I can show you where I saw the beast."

Do you believe him? Or is this just another of his lies?

To go with McFadden, turn to page 18.

To stay and search on your own, turn to page 22.

You're not sure you can trust McFadden. But this may be the only time you're ever in Scotland. If there's a chance he can help you, you have to take it. "Okay, let's take a look."

You park your car in a nearby lot and hop into McFadden's truck. The floor is littered with soda bottles, fast-food wrappers, and other garbage. You cringe, suddenly wondering if this is a good idea.

McFadden drives along a narrow, bending road. A blanket of fog has settled in over the loch, giving the place a strange, creepy feeling. McFadden turns the truck onto a little dirt road. It's barely more than two ruts carved into the ground. He pulls his truck off the road near a rocky outcropping that overlooks the loch.

"It was right about here," he says, pointing toward the water. "I saw bubbles in the water. Then a huge shadow zipped by, right below the surface. It was terrifying."

Turn to page 20.

Loch Ness stretches more than 22 miles (36 kilometers) long and is at least 700 feet (213 meters) deep in some places.

With a camera in hand, you walk out onto the rocks, following a path down to the shoreline. For an hour, you and McFadden move up and down the shore, scanning the water. "There's nothing here," you finally say. "This was a waste of time."

Several Nessie sightings have taken place as people explored the lake's rocky shore.

You head back up to the truck. But just as you're about to get in, you take one last look down. That's when you see it. Something is in the water—something big. A huge dark shape hangs just below the water's surface. In a rush, you grab your camera and snap off some images.

Click! Click! Click!

But you're too far away. The heavy fog is too thick to get a clear photo.

"It's moving!" McFadden shouts.

To rush back down to the shoreline for a closer look, turn to page 25.

To keep trying to get a decent photograph from here, turn to page 34.

"No thanks," you answer as politely as you can. You don't trust this man. Not after his big lie about the photo.

McFadden's shoulders slump. He shakes his head. "All right. I don't blame you. Whatever you decide to do, I wish you the best of luck."

With that, McFadden is gone. You sit in your car, mind racing. What if he was telling the truth? You came all this way. You might as well keep searching. You turn the car around and head back toward Loch Ness.

McFadden may have staged a hoax. But that doesn't mean Nessie isn't out there. You've come all this way. You may as well do your own searching.

But where to start? You drive along the shoreline of the loch, but the lake is huge. Your mind mulls over the problem as you drive. What do past Nessie sightings have in common? Where have big searches in the past focused their efforts?

As you drive through a small town, a sign catches your eye: BOAT RENTALS. You pull the car over, your mind racing.

A woman approaches. "Do you need a boat?" she asks in a thick accent. "The fish are biting today!"

Turn the page.

Loch Ness is a popular fishing destination during the summer months. People can rent boats to go fishing on the lake.

Renting a boat would allow you to cover a lot more area. But if you do manage to find Nessie, do you really want to be in a small boat? The idea sends a shiver down your spine.

To rent a boat and search on the water, turn to page 27.

To continue your search by land, turn to page 29.

"Let's go!" you shout. McFadden is as excited as you are. Together, you scramble back down to the shore. You're afraid you'll be too late. But to your delight, the shadow is still there.

You fire off a series of snapshots. The fog makes it hard to make out any details. All you can really see is a dark shape in the water.

Then, just like that, the creature disappears into the depths. You wait there for the rest of the day, hoping it will return. But it never does.

Later, back at McFadden's shop, you look at the photos on McFadden's computer. You definitely got images of something. But what is it? Is this enough evidence to prove that Nessie is real?

Turn the page.

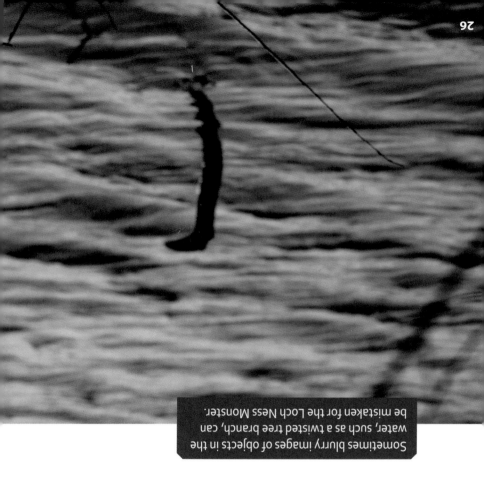

Sometimes blurry images of objects in the water, such as a twisted tree branch, can be mistaken for the Loch Ness Monster.

"We could doctor up those photos," McFadden suggests, opening up an image editor on his computer. "Make them look better."

To alter the photos, turn to page 31.

To post the photos as they are, turn to page 33.

If you want to find proof that the Loch Ness Monster exists, searching on the water seems like your best bet. You follow the woman inside to pay for one of her small motorboats. You also rent some scuba gear in case you want to go in for a better look. Then you pack up the equipment you've brought—including a small underwater drone—and head out.

The boat isn't much. Just a 12-foot wooden hull with a small motor. But it gets the job done. Within minutes, you're skipping across the water, scanning the surface for any hint of what might lie beneath.

You're not far from a section of the loch where several people have reported sightings of Nessie. There's a network of caves below the water. Some people think Nessie might call the caves home.

Turn the page.

In 2016, a previously unknown cave or trench that is nearly 900 feet (274 m) deep was discovered at the bottom of Loch Ness.

Of course, to get there, you'll have to dive. The idea of finding a sea monster deep below the water's surface makes you more than a little nervous. Should you go down yourself? Or would your underwater drone be a safer choice?

To put on the scuba gear and dive, turn to page 30.

To stay in the boat and use your drone, turn to page 36.

You shake your head. A boat would help you cover more ground, but you're a lot more comfortable on land. You decide to keep driving along the coast, searching for the perfect spot to take video of the loch. As you drive, you notice the crumbling ruins of a castle overlooking the water. It's beautiful. You pull over to snap some photographs.

A blanket of fog hangs over the water here, making for a beautiful backdrop. Then you see something. As you look out over the water, you see a dark shape moving. Your heart pounds. What is it?

To climb one of the castle walls for a better look, turn to page 41.

To rush down to the shoreline, turn to page 43.

You've come this far. There's no reason to stop now. The small boat rocks as you pull on your scuba gear. With a splash, you jump in.

The loch is cold. It takes your breath away for a moment. But you collect yourself and start your search. With a light in hand, you begin to descend. You spot the mouth of a large cave below you. As you look at it, a dark shape passes in front of the cave opening and disappears inside.

Your heart races. What was that? You couldn't make out any details. Was it just a really big fish? Or was it—something else?

To follow the shape into the cave, turn to page 38.
To wait here to see if it reappears, turn to page 40.

You hate the idea of being part of a lie. But these photos just aren't good enough. They're not proof. You know what you saw. What's the harm in fixing them up a little bit?

McFadden gets to work. He uses his editing software to make the shadow clearer. He even gives it a bit of shape, so it looks like a monster under the surface.

"Looks good," you say. With a deep breath, you log onto the cryptid message board and post the images.

It doesn't take long for people to reply.

"These are fakes!"

"Ha ha! What a terrible editing job!"

"How could anyone think that these are real?"

Turn the page.

Your lie has been exposed. You'll never be taken seriously again. Your career as a cryptid hunter is over.

THE END

To read another adventure, turn to page 9.
To learn more about lake monsters, turn to page 103.

Many people claim to have taken photos of the Loch Ness Monster. But most images have either been proven to be fakes or are too blurry to prove that the creature is real.

You roll your eyes. "No, I'm not posting any fake photos. Let's put what we've got on the message board. We'll let others decide if this is proof of Nessie."

Your photos cause a big stir in the cryptid community. A few TV stations feature them in short news segments. A few scientists even debate whether the photos are proof of Scotland's most famous mysterious creature. But in the end, the public isn't convinced.

The search for the Loch Ness Monster will have to go on.

THE END

To read another adventure, turn to page 9.
To learn more about lake monsters, turn to page 103.

"Quick!" McFadden shouts at you urgently. "Take a picture!"

In a rush, you grab your camera and scurry toward the edge of the rock outcropping. As you run toward the water, you try to aim and focus the camera.

This is it! You're going to get a picture of Nessie! Your heart is racing as you get ready to take the shot. But the dense fog has left the rocks wet and slippery. As you stop to take your shot, your feet slip out from under you. You fall awkwardly onto the rocks and land with a crack, twisting your ankle.

"Aaaagghh!" you cry out as pain shoots up your leg. But you quickly put the pain aside. This is your one chance to get proof. Your camera crashed down next to you. You quickly grab it and lift it to your face.

Some sightings of Nessie may actually be of large fish called sturgeon or giant eels that live in the lake.

But your heart sinks. You see that the lens is cracked. You and McFadden can only look on helplessly as the dark shape fades into the depths of Loch Ness.

This was your one big chance, and you blew it.

THE END

To read another adventure, turn to page 9.
To learn more about lake monsters, turn to page 103

As much as you want to find Nessie, you're not sure meeting the beast underwater is what you had in mind. Why not let technology do the work? You connect the drone to your phone and set it into the water.

The little drone drops below the surface and shines a dim cone of light in front of it. For 15 minutes, you search along the loch's bottom near a series of underwater caves. Just when you're about to give up, an image on the screen catches your eye. It's a large dark shape—and it's moving.

You steer the drone in for a closer look, making sure your phone is capturing the video. "Just a little closer," you mutter to yourself.

And then it happens. The shape suddenly shifts direction. It's headed straight for the drone! It all happens so fast that you're not even sure what you see.

The final frame shows an open mouth filled with rows of razor-sharp teeth. And then you lose contact with the drone.

Was the creature a big fish? Or was it a legendary sea monster? You can't wait to upload the video to the message board. But will it be enough to prove Nessie's existence? Only time will tell.

THE END

To read another adventure, turn to page 9.
To learn more about lake monsters, turn to page 103.

Very little light reaches
the bottom of Loch Ness.

You're so focused on finding Nessie that you
don't even consider the danger of going into the
cave. As you swim through the opening, you're
wrapped in darkness. The narrow beam of your
light does little to help show the way.

The cave twists and turns. At one point, you think you might see a shape up ahead. You follow it, only to find a dead end.

Your air tank is getting low. It's time to head back to the surface. You turn around, but realize you don't know which way to go. A sense of panic grips you as you try to follow the twists and turns back outside. You're lost! Which way is out?

Your air tank is down to 5 percent. You're running out of time, and there's no way out. This cave may be Nessie's home. And now it's about to become your watery grave.

THE END

To read another adventure, turn to page 9.
To learn more about lake monsters, turn to page 103.

Going inside the cave would be a terrible risk. You could get trapped or lost. No. You'll stay where you are and hope the shape returns. You wait and watch as long as you can. But nothing appears. After a while, you have to resurface before running out of air.

In the boat, you swap out your oxygen tanks and head back down. But it's hopeless. You don't see another hint of Nessie. As the sun drops low in the sky, you realize it's time to head back.

This search has been a failure. But you're not going to give up. Maybe tomorrow you'll have better luck.

THE END

To read another adventure, turn to page 9.
To learn more about lake monsters, turn to page 103.

A higher vantage point might help you get a better view. A crumbling staircase leads up along one of the old walls. You rush up, taking the stairs two at a time. The castle's roof is long gone, and a large hole in the wall leads to a narrow ledge that overlooks the loch.

The ruins of Urquhart Castle provide a great view of Loch Ness.

Turn the page.

You step out onto the ledge, peering out toward the water. The shape is still there! You bring your camera up to take a shot, inching out farther onto the ledge as you do.

CRACK!

The old stone gives way. Suddenly, you're falling. Below you lies only large rocks and jagged rubble from the collapsed wall.

This is not going to end well.

THE END

To read another adventure, turn to page 9.
To learn more about lake monsters, turn to page 103.

Without hesitating, you rush down toward the shoreline. The fog swallows you up as you reach the water. You can't see much at all. Desperately, you scan the water, searching for some sign of movement.

Then it appears. A large shape heaves up out of the water, just in front of you. With lightning-quick reflexes, you snap off several photos.

But as fast as you are, the creature is faster. Just as quickly as it appeared, it's gone. Your photos aren't great. The beast moved too fast, and the camera lens was damp from the fog. It's hard to make out exactly what you saw. But there's no doubt, you've got something here. It just might be the evidence needed to prove that something ancient really lurks below the waters of Loch Ness.

THE END

To read another adventure, turn to page 9.
To learn more about lake monsters, turn to page 103.

Lake Champlain lies on the border between Quebec, Canada, and the states of New York and Vermont.

CHAPTER 3

IN SEARCH OF CHAMP

You don't have to travel across the ocean to find proof of an ancient lake monster. Lake Champlain has its own famous monster. People have been seeing a strange, huge creature there for more than 100 years. It's time to start your own search for Champ.

After your plane touches down in Plattsburgh, New York, you rent a car and start your search. Lake Champlain, nestled in the Adirondack Mountains, is beautiful. Lush green forests surround the still blue waters.

Thousands of tourists flock to the lake every year to enjoy the scenery. But you're not here for a vacation. You're here to get to work.

Turn the page.

You drive to a small campground that lies along the lake. This is where the grainy video of Champ was taken. A few tents are set up on the grounds, but you don't see many people around. A young man is emptying nearby trash cans.

"Hello," you call out.

The young man looks up and smiles. "Welcome! I'm Julio. Interested in renting a campsite for the weekend?"

"Thanks, but no," you answer. You don't know how long you'll be staying here. "I'm actually following up on a video that was recorded near here."

Julio laughs. "Ahh, you're here to hunt for our famous Champ! You've come to the right place. The creature's been spotted here at least three times this year.

"The water's that way," Julio says, pointing. "Be sure to get a picture if you see it!"

"Thanks, I'll do that," you say. With that, Julio gets back to work. You grab your backpack, loaded with cameras, a drone, and other supplies, and hike down to the shore.

It's a big lake. As you gaze up and down the shore, you realize that you've got a lot of ground to cover. Should you just start walking and keep your eyes on the water? Or should you let technology do the work for you?

To start hiking, turn to page 48.

To use your drone to explore, turn to page 50.

Lake Champlain is surrounded by beautiful mountain scenery and rocky shorelines.

It's a beautiful day for a hike. If you're going to search, why not get some exercise while you're at it? You walk along the shoreline, listening to the birds. There's no wind, and the water is glassy smooth. You take some pictures of the scenery as you go, but there's no sign of a lake monster.

The rough dirt trail you've been following comes to an end, but you continue along the shore. You carefully work your way around a rocky outcropping and move back into the edge of the dense forest.

CRACK!

Suddenly, a loud snap of breaking branches stops you in your tracks. You hear a low, chuffing sound of something breathing—something big.

A moose stands between you and the shore. It's only about 40 feet from you. Too close for comfort. If the giant animal decides to charge, you'll be in serious trouble.

To wave your arms and shout
to scare away the beast, turn to page 52.

To turn and run, turn to page 54.

You knew the lake was big. But you didn't realize just how big it is. You can cover a lot more ground with a drone than you can on foot. Besides, you're excited to try out your newest toy.

You take a few minutes to set up the drone and link it to your cell phone. Then with the tap of a button, the drone lifts up into the air. The controls are a little fussy at first, but you quickly get the hang of it. Soon you're sending the drone soaring along the shoreline of the lake. The drone's camera sends video back to your phone. You watch for anything out of the ordinary.

It doesn't take long. Not far down the shore, you notice an odd dark shape near a large cluster of rocks jutting out of the water. It may be nothing, but you have to check it out. You bring the drone back in and head for the campground.

The camp rents kayaks. So you quickly pay for one and head out to explore the rocks. As you approach the area where you saw the shape, you get uneasy. What if there really is a monster just under the water? The thought is pretty terrifying.

To observe the rocks from a distance, turn to page 58.

To get closer to the rocks, turn to page 59.

An adult male moose can be more than 7 feet (2.1 m) tall at the shoulder and weigh more than 1,400 pounds (635 kilograms).

"Aaahhhh!" you scream, waving your arms and trying to look as big as you can. You hope the moose will just run away. But your actions have the opposite effect. The spooked animal charges instead!

With shocking speed, the moose barrels through the brush, lowering its huge antlers. They slam into you with terrible force, sending you flying back toward the rocky outcropping.

CRACK! SNAP!

You can hear your ribs breaking as you slam down onto the rocks. You lie there in pain as the animal retreats. You can barely breathe. You feel yourself losing consciousness.

That's when you see it. Something huge rises out of the water. Are you having a hallucination? Or is this really Champ, right in front of you?

You lift your phone. You have only seconds before you pass out. What should you do?

To call for help, turn to page 62.
To take a picture of Champ, turn to page 64.

Your instincts kick in, and you quickly turn and run. It's a good thing too, as you hear the moose chuffing and snorting behind you. It's about to charge.

You dive for cover behind the trunk of a huge oak tree—just in time. The moose barrels past you, its head lowered. Luckily, it just keeps running into the forest and out of sight.

You let out a big breath. "That was too close," you mutter to yourself.

You take a few moments to calm your racing heart and then head back to the shore. To the west you notice some tall dark clouds. It looks like a thunderstorm might be rolling in.

Animals often create trails through grass and plants next to lakes as they go to get water.

But that's not the only thing that catches your eye. Far ahead, along the shore, you notice a spot where the tall grass and bushes are trampled. Does Champ ever come ashore? If so, could this be the monster's trail?

To return to the campground before the storm hits, turn to page 56.

To investigate the trampled brush, turn to page 70.

You've already had your share of adventure for the day. No need to risk getting caught out in a thunderstorm. You decide to head back, working your way along the shoreline. You keep your eyes open for signs of Champ, but you don't see a hint of the beast.

Before long the wind starts to howl. A crack of thunder rattles your bones. The storm is coming in fast, and you're still at least half a mile from the campground.

You feel a few droplets of rain. Then the sky opens up. It's pouring. A bolt of lightning flashes across the lake. You scan your surroundings and spot a large hollow opening in a nearby tree. You might be able to shelter inside. But you have no idea how long the storm might last.

To sprint back to camp in the storm, turn to page 65.
To take shelter in the tree, turn to page 68.

A large hollow tree can be useful for shelter in an emergency.

Your nerves get the best of you. It's better to watch safely from a distance than risk a close encounter with an unknown creature. Storm clouds are gathering to the west as well, so you'll want to keep an eye on them. You don't want to be caught out on the water in a thunderstorm.

You spend the next 30 minutes watching and waiting. Several times you notice ripples on the water's surface. Then you think you see a shadow appear to dart across the water. Was it a passing cloud—or something beneath the surface?

Your heart is racing. Are you getting close or just wasting your time? The sound of distant thunder tells you that the clock is ticking.

To get a closer look, go to page 59.
To play it safe and paddle for shore, turn to page 72.

You paddle closer to the rocks. This is too thrilling. You continue taking photos of the water, focusing on every shadow and ripple you see. One shadow looks a lot like, well, a sea monster. Could this be the proof you've come to find? You shoot photos as fast as you can.

Suddenly a bright flash of lightning cuts through the sky. BOOM! The crack of thunder rattles your kayak.

Strong storms on open water can be very dangerous.

Turn the page.

The storm is bearing down on you. It's not safe to be out on the water. You've got some images on your camera. Who knows? Maybe when you get back, you'll find the magic shot that proves Champ is real.

You put away the camera and start paddling back toward the campground. But before you're halfway back, the skies open up. It starts pouring rain. Gusts of wind kick up big waves that rock your little kayak.

You're not sure you can make it back. You need to act fast.

To head to shore to wait out the storm, go to page 61.

To try to make it back to
the campground, turn to page 72.

You'll never make it back to the campground in this storm. You dig hard for the shore and finally run the kayak aground on a rocky beach. You drag the little boat away from the water's edge and run for the cover of the forest.

You spot a large tree with a hollowed-out trunk. It's not the best shelter in a storm, but it's better than nothing.

Turn to page 68.

The world is spinning. You know you don't have time to take a picture. You need help. You manage to tap the phone icon and dial 911.

"911, what is your emergency?" answers a voice on the other end.

"Help me," you mutter. "Moose attack . . . I'm losing . . ."

You can't finish the sentence. The darkness creeps in, and you pass out. But you're in luck. The 911 operator is able to locate your phone with GPS. Paramedics arrive and rush you to the hospital. You're in rough shape, but you're going to survive.

You'll always wonder about what you saw. Was it real? Or was your mind just playing tricks on you?

Search and rescue teams provide first aid to help people injured in the wilderness.

It will be a while before you can go on another hunt for Champ. But you vow to try again.

Maybe next time, you'll get the proof you're after.

THE END

To read another adventure, turn to page 9.
To learn more about lake monsters, turn to page 103.

You lift the phone and open the camera app. You manage to snap a few photos of the shoreline before you finally black out.

Unfortunately, nobody knows where you are. Help is not on the way. In your final moments, you tried to capture proof that Champ is real. Did you get the shot? Was the creature even there, or was it a figment of your imagination? And if beast was real, will anyone ever bother to look at your phone to see what you captured?

One thing is certain. Your search is over. Was it worth it?

THE END

To read another adventure, turn to page 9.
To learn more about lake monsters, turn to page 103.

You need to get out of this storm. You've got to run for it. You stick close to the shore, where the ground is free of brush. But as you leap over a large boulder, your foot slips on the wet ground. You crash to the ground in a heap and bang your head.

For a moment, you see stars. You sit there, stunned, staring out at the water as the rain pours down. That's when you see it. Some type of dark shape is moving across the water. You can see its wake breaking behind it.

"Champ!" you shout out loud. You scramble to grab your camera and fire off a series of photos. As the dark shape disappears in the distance, you eagerly look at the shots you've taken.

Turn the page.

As you zoom in, you prepare yourself. What will Champ look like? How much detail did you capture in the pouring rain?

That's when your heart sinks. The dark shape isn't Champ at all. It's just a boat hurrying toward shore to get out of the storm.

In stormy weather, it can be difficult to see objects in the distance clearly.

You're soaking wet with a lump on your head, and you just took pictures of a boat. What a failure. Maybe this cryptid hunting business just isn't for you.

THE END

To read another adventure, turn to page 9.
To learn more about lake monsters, turn to page 103.

You can't stay out here in this downpour. Sheltering inside a tree during a lightning storm isn't the greatest idea, but you don't have much choice. So you curl yourself up and crawl inside.

It's cool and damp, but at least you're out of the rain. You watch as the storm sweeps across the lake, dumping rain in sheets. Lightning lights up the sky, and the thunder is deafening.

But one creature isn't bothered by the weather. Tucked away inside the hollow of the tree, you spot it gliding across the middle of the lake. "It's Champ," you whisper to yourself as you scoop up your camera.

It's tough to get a perfect shot. Champ is a long way off. And the heavy rain and fog make details hard to make out. But there's no doubt in your mind. This is what you came for.

An artist's concept of what Champ may look like

Will the images you capture convince everyone that Champ is real? You hope so. One thing is certain. You're about to become the most famous cryptozoologist in the world!

THE END

To read another adventure, turn to page 9.
To learn more about lake monsters, turn to page 103.

The clouds are still on the horizon. You think you have enough time to investigate the area a little more. You move on until you reach the trampled brush.

"This is strange," you say as you look at the flattened bushes and small trees. If you use your imagination, you can almost see the path made by a large animal from the water to the edge of the forest.

Thunder cracks as you kneel down to look at a strange print in the ground. It's at least half a yard wide. What could have made it? You continue on until you see something that stops you in your tracks. It's a nest. Nestled inside are three eggs the size of watermelons.

You gasp and reach for your camera. Then another booming sound fills the air. But this isn't thunder. It's more like a roar!

You whirl around just in time to see it. A huge shadow falls over you. Too late, you realize your mistake. You always thought Champ was male. But the creature is really a female. And you just got between a mother and her nest!

The good news is that you found what you were looking for. The bad news is that nobody will ever find you or hear your amazing tale.

THE END

To read another adventure, turn to page 9.
To learn more about lake monsters, turn to page 103.

Storms with high winds can create big waves and dangerous conditions for anyone in a small boat.

As you start paddling back, the storm front hits. A blast of wind kicks up huge waves that rock your kayak. You struggle to make any headway in the strong wind. Then a huge whitecap slams into the side of the little boat.

There's nothing you can do. The kayak tips over, and you splash into the chilly water with a splash. Too late, you realize your camera has slipped off your neck. It sinks to the bottom of the deep lake, taking all of the photos you'd captured with it.

You manage to climb back onto the kayak and struggle to shore. You're safe, but you're defeated. You're cold and wet. And worst of all, you've lost your camera and all of your photos. It's time to go home. You have a wild tale to tell, but no proof of Champ.

THE END

To read another adventure, turn to page 9.
To learn more about lake monsters, turn to page 103.

The Congo River flows for about
2,900 miles (4,700 km) through
the jungles of Africa.

CHAPTER 4

A CONGO ADVENTURE

You've always wanted to travel to Africa. The Congo River is said to be home to a long-necked, long-tailed monster the size of an elephant. The stories about Mokele-mbembe fascinate you. If there's a chance it's real, you want to be the one to find it. You book your flight and pack your bags for an African adventure.

While you're on the long flight, you dive into research on the strange creature. The latest report comes from a small village that lies along the banks of the Congo River. According to the villagers, Mokele-mbembe spends part of its time in the water and part on land. That could make the search easier.

Turn the page.

Your small plane touches down at N'djili Airport in the Democratic Republic of Congo. As you step off the plane, an airport security officer, Emmanual, asks where you're going. He speaks with a thick accent, but his English is good. You tell him about your search for Mokele-mbembe.

Emmanual's face grows stern. "Maybe you should turn around," he says. "What you want to do . . . it is dangerous."

But you're not giving up that easily. "No, I want to go. I can rent a car. How do I get there?"

The man shakes his head. "No. You cannot drive there. This village is small. Far from the city. You will need a guide. My brother, Moise. He knows this area. He speaks English. If you pay him, he will take you."

You agree, relieved for any help you can get.

Emmanual tells you to wait outside the airport. Within an hour, Moise arrives. He drives an old, beat-up pickup truck. "Get in," he says. You toss your bag in the back and hop inside. As Moise drives out of the city, the two of you chat about Mokele-mbembe.

"Yes, everyone here knows about it," he says. He shares stories about the huge monster that strikes fear into all the children who live near the river.

"I've never seen the monster myself," Moise goes on. "But it will be exciting to find him together!"

After a few hours, you're rumbling along a dirt road that leads to the most recent sighting. The monster is said to live both on land and in the water. Where should you look first?

To explore the nearby jungle, turn to page 78.
To search the Congo River, turn to page 80.

"Many of the reports of Mokele-mbembe
are from swampy areas near the river," you tell
Moise. "Let's search along the lowlands near the
river. If the creature is as big as reports say, it
will be hard to miss."

The two of you continue on foot into the
dense jungle. Mosquitoes buzz all around you.
The air is hot and humid, and it doesn't take
long before you're soaked in sweat.

"I hear water," Moise says. He stops,
listening carefully.

"Yes, I hear it too," you reply. "That way!"

The two of you trek through the heavy
brush to a swamp. A small stream and waterfall
spills into the wet lowland. Large, moss-covered
boulders jut out of the swamp.

Small streams and waterfalls are common in rain forests.

It's beautiful. But as you lift your camera to take a photo, something catches your eye. Did that boulder just move? Or was it your imagination?

To wade into the swamp for a closer look, turn to page 82.

To climb to the top of the waterfall for a better view, turn to page 86.

You've come all this way to explore the Congo River. That's where you'll start. Moise leads you into a small village that lies along the mighty Congo. It's a remote place. Some of the people here have never seen a real outsider. You get some strange looks as you enter the village.

Moise asks a young man about the latest Mokele-mbembe sighting. The man answers eagerly. He points and gestures toward the river. Moise translates for you.

"He says that two men were fishing just half a kilometer downstream from here," Moise says. "They saw a massive beast rise out of the water and disappear into the jungle."

You thank the young man and head to the place where the men reported seeing Mokele-mbembe. The banks of the Congo are thick with brush.

"Keep your eyes open for crocodiles and hippos," Moise warns. "Many people come to Africa thinking lions will kill them. But hippos and crocs are more dangerous."

You reach the correct spot. It's a gentle bend in the huge river. In one direction, a low wetland lies along the banks. Thick reeds there could easily hide a large animal. A little farther ahead, a rocky cliff rises up to overlook the river.

To explore the rocky cliff, turn to page 88.
To head for the reeds, turn to page 97.

"Did you see that?" Moise asks.

You nod. "I did. I don't know what it is, but I'm going to get a closer look."

"Do not go into the swamp," Moise says. But you're already waist-deep in the warm, muddy water. With a sigh, Moise follows you. The two of you move through the swamp slowly. Your feet stick in the mud with every step.

You draw closer to the boulder or whatever it is. Mokele-mbembe is supposed to be the size of an elephant, but this is quite a bit smaller. Could it be a young one?

That's when you realize your mistake. It's not Mokele-mbembe. It's something that may be far more dangerous.

"Hippo!" Moise shouts. "RUN!"

Adult male hippos can weigh as much as 8,000 pounds (3,600 kg)! They are often aggressive toward humans.

To run toward the waterfall, turn to page 84.

To run back toward the jungle, turn to page 92.

You don't waste any time. The waterfall is closer, so you slosh in that direction as fast as you can. Moise is right behind you. You can hear his panicked breathing as you slog through the heavy mud. A look over your shoulder shows you that the hippo is closing—fast.

With every bit of strength you have, you surge ahead. You scramble up onto a group of high rocks and keep climbing. You reach back to grab Moise's hand and haul him up to safety behind you.

You both flop down on the rock, breathing heavily. Lucky for you both, the hippo gives up and heads back into the swap.

"That was close," you say.

"What, you never ran from a hippo before?" Moise jokes. You both break out laughing.

After you catch your breath, you decide to head up the waterfall to see what you can see.

A high waterfall plunges down as water flows through a river in Africa.

Turn the page.

The rocks along the waterfall are wet and slippery, but you and Moise manage to claw your way to the top. The view from up here is amazing. Swampy lowlands lie in one direction. The dense jungle stretches out before you in the other.

A group of a dozen or so hippos lingers in the swamp. But there's no sign of anything bigger.

Hippos spend most of their time in the water. They usually only travel onto land to find food.

In the opposite direction, a wide stream winds through the thick jungle. The lush green jungle makes it easy to imagine seeing some kind of huge Jurassic-age beast here.

"Let's look that way," Moise suggests, pointing toward the stream. You're quick to agree.

You follow along the stream until you come to what appears to be a large game path. Animals have carved it into the jungle as they visit the stream to drink.

"Which way?" Moise asks.

To follow the game path, turn to page 93.
To continue along the stream, turn to page 95.

There's no telling what might be lurking in those tall reeds. It's not a risk you're willing to take. "Up there," you tell Moise, pointing to the cliff. "We can see in every direction up on those rocks. It will be a perfect spot to watch the water."

Your rock-climbing skills are rusty, and Moise has clearly never climbed a rock in his life. After a series of slips, stumbles, and scrapes, the two of you manage to claw your way to the top of the cliff. It's a beautiful spot. The river flows by below you, and the jungle stretches in every direction. People describe Mokele-mbembe as a dinosaur-like creature. It's not hard to imagine some Jurassic beast lumbering through this wilderness.

You spend the afternoon watching. But as the day stretches into evening and the light begins to fade, you know your time is short.

"There!" Moise shouts, pointing to the riverbank. Something large is moving among the shadows. Quickly, you snap a few shots with your camera. But the lighting is just too dim. You're not sure the photos are going to show any detail at all.

"Should we go down there?" you whisper.

Moise shakes his head. "No way. I'm staying right here."

To go down alone to get a closer look, turn to page 90.
To continue taking pictures
from the safety of the rocks, turn to page 101.

There's something down there, and you have to know what it is. You put the camera strap around your neck and carefully climb down.

"Be careful!" Moise whispers.

Then everything goes wrong. A rock breaks away under your foot and you fall—right into the river below! With a splash, you slam into the warm water. Your camera flies off your neck and sinks out of reach.

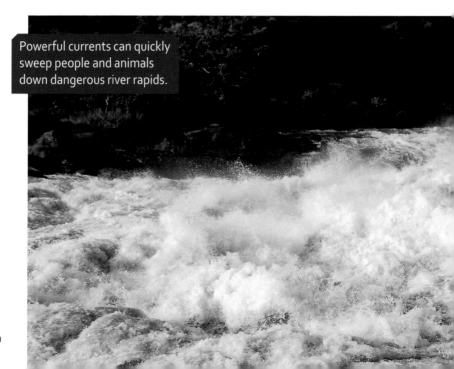

Powerful currents can quickly sweep people and animals down dangerous river rapids.

But right now you're not worried about your camera or about finding Mokele-mbembe. You're being swept away by the river's strong current!

To try to swim to shore, turn to page 99.

To just keep your head above water as the current carries you, turn to page 100.

You turn and run as fast as you can back the way you came. Hippos are huge. You're sure you can outrun it.

But you've made a terrible mistake. Running through the mud is like running in slow motion. Moise is a little faster than you. He pulls ahead. But the hippo is much faster than both of you. You can hear it closing on you. Then, you can almost feel its hot breath on your neck.

When it slams into you, everything goes dark. Hippos are very aggressive. They will attack anything that they see as a threat. Today, that means you. You don't have a chance against such a massive and powerful beast. Your search for Mokele-mbembe is over.

THE END

To read another adventure, turn to page 9.
To learn more about water monsters, turn to page 103.

"That way," you say, pointing toward the game trail.

You follow the trail through the jungle. It's narrow—too small to have been made by anything as big as Mokele-mbembe. But maybe it'll lead you to something bigger.

Turn the page.

Wild animals often travel the same path through a forest or jungle to create an easy-to-follow trail.

After 30 minutes of following the winding, forking trail, you're lost. "We came from that way," Moise says.

"No, it was that direction," you insist. But the truth is, neither of you are certain.

Just then, you hear a rustling in the trees above you. Your first thought is that Mokele-mbembe might be lurking nearby. But you're not so lucky. Instead, a leopard leaps down onto the path before you. The big cat shows you its sharp teeth—and it looks hungry.

Moise reacts more quickly than you. He's already running in the other direction. You turn and follow. But you can't outrun a leopard. You can only hope that it's a quick end.

THE END

To read another adventure, turn to page 9.
To learn more about water monsters, turn to page 103.

Mokele-mbembe may spend some of its time on land, but it's a water creature. You need to stay near water if you hope to find it. So you stick to the stream.

You follow along the water until you come to a clearing in the jungle. On the far side of the clearing, something is moving—something big.

"It's the monster," Moise whispers.

You grab your camera and start snapping photos. Unfortunately, you can't get a clear shot through the thick trees. But you can tell the beast is big. If you use your imagination, you think you can see a long dinosaur-like neck.

After a few minutes, the creature disappears into the jungle. Your heart is racing. Have you done it? Are your photos enough to prove that a strange, ancient animal lurks in the Congo Basin?

Turn the page.

Only time will tell. For now, you need to
get back to civilization to upload your amazing
photos. You know that with evidence like
this, you're about to become the talk of the
cryptozoology community.

THE END

To read another adventure, turn to page 9.
To learn more about water monsters, turn to page 103.

Could a creature like Mokele-mbembe be hiding in the swamps and wetlands of Africa's jungles?

"That way," you tell Moise. The low wetland looks like the perfect environment for a mysterious, large creature.

The ground here is wet and muddy. Your boots sink into the mud up to your ankles as you trudge into the thick reeds. Swamp water rises to your waist. Insects buzz all around you, biting and stinging you every chance they get. Within a few minutes, you get the feeling that this wasn't a great idea.

But the bugs are only the beginning. Something much larger is lurking nearby. Suddenly, you hear the snapping of reeds. A huge monster bursts out of the heavy brush! It's on you in a heartbeat, grabbing and pulling you under the shallow water. You hear Moise shouting as you feel the air rush from your lungs.

Turn the page.

You came to Africa to find a monster—and you found one. Unfortunately for you, it wasn't the fabled Mokele-mbembe. It was a huge, hungry crocodile. Your African adventure has come to a gruesome end.

Adult crocodiles can grow to about 16 feet (4.9 m) long and weigh about 500 pounds (227 kg). They have one of the most powerful bites in the world.

THE END

To read another adventure, turn to page 9.
To learn more about water monsters, turn to page 103.

You have to act fast. The current is strong, and it could sweep you far downstream in just few minutes. You swim as hard as you can toward the shore. It's a battle. Your clothes weigh you down. But you don't panic. You remain calm and put every ounce of strength into the swim.

When you finally reach the bank and your feet touch ground, you feel an amazing sense of relief. You pull yourself onto the muddy bank and collapse. Soon you hear Moise shouting as he rushes down toward you.

Your camera is gone, along with any images that you might have captured. But you're alive. And if you're feeling up to it, you can hunt for Mokele-mbembe another day.

THE END

To read another adventure, turn to page 9.
To learn more about water monsters, turn to page 103.

All you can do right now is try to keep your head above water. The current sweeps you along for what seems like forever. Finally, as the river approaches a bend, the current weakens. You manage to paddle toward a rocky bank and drag yourself out of the water.

The shadows are long. It's going to be dark soon. Moise doesn't know where you are, and you don't know how to get back. The wild jungle is filled with leopards, crocodiles, hippos, and other deadly creatures.

Your search for Mokele-mbembe is over for now. You'll never stop fighting. But you know that you'll be lucky to survive the night.

THE END

To read another adventure, turn to page 9.
To learn more about water monsters, turn to page 103.

Moise is right. You're safe up here. As badly as you want to take a closer look, finding Mokele-mbembe isn't worth losing your life. So you keep snapping photos.

The big figure—whatever it is—remains cloaked in shadows. Finally, it disappears into the trees.

"Was that it?" you ask Moise.

He shrugs his shoulders and shakes his head. "I don't know. But the sun will set soon. We need to get back."

You can't stop smiling as the two of you hike back to the truck. Did you find absolute proof that Mokele-mbembe exists? No. But you did find something odd in the jungle. You'll never forget your adventure in the jungles of Africa.

THE END

To read another adventure, turn to page 9.
To learn more about water monsters, turn to page 103.

This image taken in 1938 reportedly shows Nessie as the creature swims across the surface of Loch Ness.

CHAPTER 5

EXPLAINING LAKE MONSTERS

The idea that huge, ancient creatures lurk in the world's deepest lakes has long fascinated people. Nessie, the Loch Ness Monster, is by far the most famous of these elusive creatures. But it's not alone. Tales of giant beasts come from all over the world—from North America to Africa to Australia.

Ancient people often told tales of such monsters. But modern people still get excited at the idea of spotting one. Sometimes, that enthusiasm goes too far. Many famous photos of Nessie and other water monsters have turned out to be hoaxes.

The most famous Nessie photograph was taken in 1934 by Colonel Robert Wilson. The image appeared on the front pages of newspapers around the world. Had Wilson finally photographed the world's most famous monster? The photo fooled many people. But it was a fake. Wilson had built the "monster" out of a toy submarine. His trick was just one in a long line of Nessie hoaxes.

Wilson's 1934 photo made Nessie one of the most famous cryptid monsters in the world.

Such scams have caused many people to believe that Nessie and other lake monsters are all a lie. But others remain convinced that something unusual does live in the world's deep lakes. Some people think a small group of plesiosaurs—reptiles from the time of the dinosaurs—may have survived undetected in the lakes for millions of years. But that's just one theory. Others suggest that Nessie could actually be a large fish called a sturgeon or a giant eel.

What do you think? Is it all a hoax? Are Nessie, Champ, and their cousins just larger than usual animals such as eels or fish? Or is there something more mysterious just waiting to be found? Will we ever know for sure?

Lake Monsters Around the World

Stories of large freshwater monsters come from all over the world. The Loch Ness Monster might be the most famous of them. But Nessie is far from alone.

Loch Ness, Scotland
The Loch Ness Monster, or "Nessie"
The first recorded sighting of Nessie comes from AD 565. A man reported chasing the monster away after it bit a swimmer.

Lake Ikeda, Japan
"Issie"
A myth from Japan says that Issie was once a horse. When her foal was captured, she jumped into the water and turned into a monster. She spends her time searching for her lost foal.

Lake Champlain, United States
"Champ"
Champ is so popular that in 1983, the state of New York passed a law protecting it. A statue of the famous monster stands by the water in Port Henry, New York.

The Congo River

"Mokele-mbembe"

According to legend, Mokele-mbembe lives in caves it digs along the riverbanks. It eats elephants, hippos, and crocodiles. That's one tough monster!

Okanagan Lake, British Columbia, Canada

"Ogopogo"

This lake monster is said to tip over boats and even pull horses into the water. Some think it could be an ancient whale called a basilosaurus.

Storsjön, Sweden

"Storsjöodjuret"

This creature has a long body and neck with a doglike head. Its skin is gray-brown, while its belly is yellow. Hundreds of people have reportedly seen the ancient creature.

Lake Van, Turkey

"The Lake Van Monster"

The Lake Van Monster looks a lot like Nessie. It measures 50 feet (15 m) in length, with a long neck and tail. It might just be Nessie's distant cousin!

Glossary

consciousness (KON-shuhs-nuhs)—the state of being fully awake and aware of what's happening around you

cryptid (KRIP-tihd)—an animal or creature that people have claimed to see but has never been proven to exist

cryptozoology (krip-tuh-zoh-AH-luh-jee)—the study of evidence for unproven creatures such as Bigfoot or the Loch Ness monster

drone (DROHN)—an unmanned, remote-controlled device, often equipped with a camera

elusive (ee-LOO-siv)—clever at hiding

evidence (EV-uh-duhnss)—information, items, and facts that help prove something to be true or false

expedition (ek-spuh-DIH-shuhn)—a journey made for a specific purpose, such as exploring a new region or looking for something

GPS (GEE-pee-ess)—an electronic tool that uses signals from satellites to find a specific location; GPS stands for Global Positioning System

hallucination (huh-loo-suh-NAY-shuhn)—the experience of seeing something that is not really there

hoax (HOHKS)—a trick to make people believe something that is not true

loch (LAHK)—the Scottish word for lake

Jurassic (joo-RAS-ik)—a geologic period during which dinosaurs lived

plesiosaur (PLEE-see-uh-sohr)—a large swimming reptile that lived during the time of the dinosaurs

theory (THEE-uh-ree)—an idea that explains something that is unknown

Other Paths to Explore

>>> Some people research cryptid creatures, such as the Loch Ness Monster, full-time. But many sightings come from ordinary people. How would you feel if you caught a glimpse of one of these beasts? Would you be excited or terrified? Would you tell everyone or keep it quiet in fear that nobody would believe you?

>>> Many cryptid sightings turn out to be hoaxes. People make fake photos and videos trying to fool people into believing it's really a strange creature. How would you react to new evidence that claims these beasts are real? Would you believe whatever you see, or would you want more proof to back up the claim?

>>> Cryptids are a booming business. Imagine you own a business that relies on tourism. Reports of a sighting of Nessie, Champ, or another creature might be great for business. Would you try to encourage people to believe that the monsters are real? Or would you tell them that it could all be a hoax?

Read More

Oachs, Emily Rose. *The Loch Ness Monster.* Minneapolis: Bellwether Media, Inc., 2019.

Peabody, Erin. *The Loch Ness Monster.* New York: Little Bee Books, 2017.

Internet Sites

Loch Ness Monster Facts for Kids
kids.kiddle.co/Loch_Ness_Monster

The Legend of Loch Ness
pbs.org/wgbh/nova/article/legend-loch-ness/

Brandon Terrell (B.1978 – D.2021) Brandon was a passionate reader and Star Wars fan; amazing father and son; and devoted husband. Brandon was a talented storyteller, authoring more than 100 books for children in his career. This book is dedicated in his memory.—Happy Reading!

Matt Doeden
Matt Doeden is a freelance author and editor who has written numerous children's books on sports, music, the military, extreme survival, and much more. He began his career as a sports writer before turning to publishing. He lives in Minnesota with his wife and two children.

Index